I Didn't Speak Up

By Richard Carlson Jr.

Illustrated by Kevin Carlson

My younger brother Hoc and me, Minh

It was a cold December afternoon and snowing. A thick blanket of snow covered the ground. My little brother Hoc and I had just finished playing a board game at the kitchen table.

"How about we go to the field across from the civic center and build a huge snowman?" Dad asked Hoc and me with a big smile.

"Yippee!" Hoc cheered.

"All right," I said, and giggled because I was feeling so happy. My heart sang with joy.

We jumped down from our chairs. "Can we bring the sled?" Hoc asked. "So we can play school bus?"

"Yes," Dad said with a smile.

I wanted to play school bus, but didn't want any of my friends to see me playing it. I didn't want them to think that I was still a baby, like my brother.

Mom and Dad

Mom was feeling depressed, like she had been for weeks. I hoped she would feel better today, since it was a snow day. Maybe she'd want to snuggle in a blanket and read books and do crossword puzzles, like how she used to, when she was happy.

Mom and Dad had both told Hoc and me that it wasn't our fault Mom felt depressed. Many different things in a person's life can cause depression—some as simple as not exercising and not eating healthy. Sometimes it's more complicated than that, though. Depression often makes life difficult; Mom couldn't help with our homework sometimes, and sometimes she didn't want to play with us.

Mom and Dad helped us get dressed to go outside in the cold weather. At the field, we got out of our pickup truck and Mom opened the tailgate and took out the sled. Dad took pictures and videos of us as we played in the snow.

Hoc, Mom, and I helped each other make a huge snowman. Mom pointed to the side of the field, near a tall, evergreen tree. "Let's make it there," she said.

We rolled snowballs until they were so big we couldn't push another inch. Even though I wore boots, my toes began to get cold.

"Errrrr. I can't lift it," I said as I leaned back, trying to lift a snowball up for the snowman's body. As hard as I lifted, the snowball wouldn't even budge! Dad took a picture of me as I tried and tried.

"I'll get it," Mom said, and then lifted the snowball into place.

She made it look easy.

Mom came over with me to gather three pieces of large gravel from the side of the street. Mom kept an eye out for cars and trucks while I picked out some good ones. Dad held Hoc up as Hoc put the pieces of gravel on the face for the eyes and nose. My toes were even colder now and it bugged me, but I was having so much fun, and I didn't want to ruin it. I kept how I was feeling to myself.

"What about his mouth?" I asked Mom.

"We'll look for a curved branch on that tree," Mom said, pointing to a maple tree. Mom held up Hoc and Hoc pulled a short, dead branch off of the tree.

"You can put it on," Mom said, and Hoc handed it to me. My toes were getting colder. I still didn't tell Mom or Dad, though. I put the stick on the snowman's face, pushing it into the snow until it was firmly in place.

"What about his arms and hands?" I asked. Mom broke two dead branches off the maple tree. Hoc and I each put an arm on our snowman.

"Hooray!" Hoc cheered, jumping up. Dad took pictures of Hoc, Mom, and me standing next to the snowman. I hoped that we all looked happy.

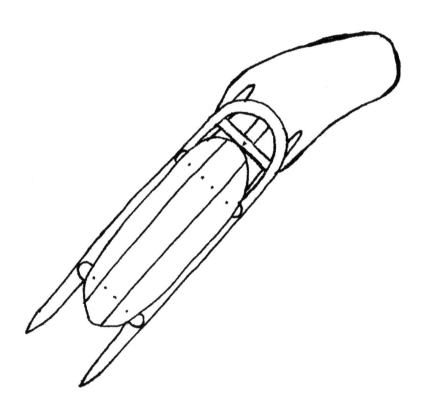

Mom pulled Hoc on the sled as he pretended it was a school bus. I threw snowballs at the snowman's back. Now, my toes were very cold. They bugged me so much that it was very uncomfortable, but I still didn't tell Mom or Dad. Dad took pictures of Hoc and Mom.

I sat on the tailgate of Dad's truck and made a sad face, looking down at my feet. No one noticed at first. My toes grew even colder and started to hurt!

Finally, Mom turned around and saw me making a sad face. "Is everything all right?" she asked. Dad and Hoc also looked at me. I had been trying to get attention, and I got it. But I still didn't tell anyone about my cold toes. I don't know why. I should have spoken up!

"No," I said in a low voice, "nothing is all right." I scowled down and kicked my feet.

"Why are you making faces? Tell us what is wrong. Now," Mom asked, her voice still nice. Dad and Hoc walked over to me.

"My toes," I said. I took a deep breath. "They're cold," I admitted sadly. Relief flooded through me and for a moment I didn't feel so bad. Maybe my toes weren't even really that cold, after all. They didn't really seem to hurt as much as I thought they did.

Why hadn't I just spoken up in the first place? I should have let my parents help me.

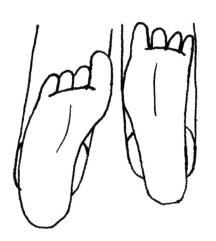

"Let me massage them," Mom said, taking off my boots and socks. "What would happen if you got frostbite?" she asked.

"I don't know," I said. "What?"

"A doctor might have to amputate your toes. That would be a shame if you lost your toes, just because you didn't tell us that you felt cold?"

"I guess," I said, looking down.

"Look at me," she said, and I did. "Do you believe that I shouldn't get help for my depression?" she asked. "What if I just sat on the sofa and looked at my lap making a sad face all of the time?"

I shrugged.

Mom did see a psychiatrist, who is a type of doctor who treats people who are depressed and have other mental illnesses. She went to her psychiatrist every now and then. The psychiatrist would ask her questions about how she is feeling and prescribe medication to help her feel well again. It sometimes took a long time for the medication to work.

"It would be ridiculous not to tell someone if you felt depressed. Then you would just keep feeling bad all the time. Tell us what's on your mind. Please," she said gently.

"Sorry," I said. I looked up at her. She was right. Just like it was dangerous to hide that my toes were getting so cold that they hurt, so it was also dangerous to hide depression. I knew that children and grown-ups who are depressed sometimes don't tell anyone and keep it a secret. At first, Mom and Dad didn't tell us about it, and it was very confusing, at times, why she was acting so different. A child who is depressed should tell a trusted parent or grown-up. Even if you keep it a secret at first, it is never too late to ask for help.

Mom asked, "Do your toes feel better?" She continued to massage them.

"They're better, now. Thank you," I said, smiling at her. Then she put my socks and boots back on.

I jumped off the tailgate and cheered, "Yippee!" I felt my heart leap.

"We'll have to get you new boots," Dad said. Then he twisted and looked down at Hoc. "How do your toes feel?" Dad asked. "Are they cold?"

"No, they're fine," he said with a smile. He tugged on the rope that pulled the sled.

"Minh, let me know if your toes get cold again," Mom said. I realized that she and Dad loved us both very much!

"All right," I said, smiling. I felt happy to be so loved.

Mom helped Hoc and I make a snowwoman and two snow children next to the snowman. Then Dad took pictures and a video of us next to the snow people. We had a great time! Mom even confided that she didn't feel as sad that day, which made us very happy.

About the Book:

In *I Didn't Speak Up,* seven-year-old Minh doesn't tell his parents about his cold toes while playing in the snow. Finally, it hurts so much that he sits down and begins to pout. Will he ever tell them what's wrong?

About the Author:

Richard Carlson Jr. is an author of children's books and coming-of-age, tween romances. He is a highly sensitive person, or HSP, and has paranoid schizophrenia and obsessive-compulsive disorder. He especially likes to provide good examples for children to follow. His stories have strong, positive role models and feature parents who are involved in their children's lives. You can learn more about him at www.rich.center.

About the Illustrator:

Kevin Carlson is a talented artist. He has autism, which is a serious brain disorder. Kevin loves art and works at a crafts store that employs mentally handicapped individuals.

Made in the USA
Las Vegas, NV
20 November 2020